GHOST IN THE CASTLE

by

William MacKellar

Illustrated by Richard Bennett

"It's feared ye are, Angus Campbell." Daft as he might be, there was no choice for him. In all of Scotland there was no lonelier place than Dunnach Moor — a wasteland of rocks and heather — but Angus was going to prove that there was or wasn't a ghost in Craigie Castle. He found a funny little man with a strange looking kilt, who told him stories of two hundred years ago as if they had happened yesterday. Was this a GHOST? Angus was put in an embarrassing position in the little village, and he had to warn his friend before the townspeople investigated the castle. Only Angus knew the truth . . .

Classification and Dewey Decimal: Fiction (Fic)

About the Author:

WILLIAM MacKELLAR came to the United States at the age of eleven from Glasgow, Scotland. During World War II he spent a furlough in Scotland revisiting childhood scenes, which he used as a background for a number of his stories. He has written many articles for teen-age magazines. An avid sports fan, Mr. MacKellar lives in Syosset, Long Island, with his wife and family.

About the Illustrator:

RICHARD BENNETT was born in County Cork, Ireland. He came to this country as a child and grew up on a ranch in the Northwest. After his graduation from the University of Washington he taught painting, but has since devoted his time to book illustrations and to writing.

GHOST
in the CASTLE

by WILLIAM MacKELLAR

Illustrated by RICHARD BENNETT

1968 FIRST CADMUS EDITION
THIS SPECIAL EDITION IS PUBLISHED BY ARRANGEMENT WITH
THE PUBLISHERS OF THE REGULAR EDITION
DAVID MCKAY COMPANY, INC.

BY

E. M. HALE AND COMPANY
EAU CLAIRE, WISCONSIN

Manufactured in the United States of America

Typography by Charles M. Todd

FOR

Wee Laurie Mary

Full Page Illustrations

GHOST IN THE CASTLE

Chapter One

The small log, rotted with fire and weary with ashes, collapsed with a soft *slushing* noise. The movement sent a column of sparks, like startled fireflies, flitting up the chimney.

Outside the cottage Angus could hear the wind skulking like a hungry beast. It sniffed at the windows and at the bottom of the door. It gnawed at the dry bones of dead leaves.

Angus felt a sudden coldness snake down his back. It was cozy in the small room. Gentle ripples of warmth swept over him from the cheery fireplace. Again he felt the skin tighten at the back of his neck. He drew his chair closer to the fire.

"A ghost? In Craigie Castle?"

He meant it to sound matter-of-fact. After all, who believed in ghosts nowadays? Yet the words hadn't come out that way. Rather they had come out soft and small and with no breath to them at all.

His great-uncle nodded. "Aye, a ghost. Or so the story has it. Right here in Craigie Castle it was too."

Angus said, "But nobody believes in ghosts any more, Uncle Wull."

"True enough," the old man said mildly. "But old Dugal Comrie was no one to believe in ghosts either." He paused. "At first."

"Old Dugal Comrie?" Angus frowned. "It's myself is no knowing the name at all."

"And with good reason, lad. He's been dead these past sixty years." Wull Campbell pushed the shreds of tobacco into the bowl of his pipe. He leaned back in his chair. "I was a wee fellow like yourself, Angus Campbell, when he first told me. Of course, Dugal was an old man then and near blind."

"And *he* was the one who saw this ghost?" Angus was conscious of the disappointment within him. It had all sounded so good in the beginning. Somehow old Dugal Comrie, and him almost blind besides, hadn't helped the story much.

"Aye he was, Angus." Wull Campbell smiled with his eyes. "Or so he said. He was an honest man, was old Dugal, though some thought a wee bit strange in his ways. I never knew him to lie though."

"H-m-m," said Angus. "No one else see him?" he asked hopefully.

Uncle Wull shrugged and poked at the fire. "There were stories. Old stories going back to old times." The flames he had poked to life cast a red glow against his face.

"A ghost?" Again Angus said the words. Again he felt the coldness suddenly shiver down his back. He was grateful for the warmth from the fire. "It's daft!" he cried loudly, angrily.

Uncle Wull rested his pipe against his heavy lower lip. "Aye, like enough," he said mildly.

"Ghosts are only in books! Everybody knows that!"

Uncle Wull said carefully, "There will be a lot of things in books. Aye, and some I'm no doubting are true things."

Angus said nothing. He wasn't really annoyed any more that old Dugal Comrie had somehow spoiled a good story. After all, this was the part of the day that he liked best. When the work was done and the supper cleared from the table. How often they had sat there, the two of them! A whole lifetime it seemed. Yet it had only been since that black day, the day when the villagers had stood mute at the door with pain in their eyes. That day his fisherman father had gone out on the black waters of Loch Lorne and had not returned. He was suddenly aware of the rise and fall of Uncle Wull's voice in his ears.

"—aye, many there were even then that laughed at old Dugal Comrie. Called him a daft old soul with no sense in him at all. And maybe it's right they were. But old Dugal, he just smiled at them. Just smiled and said he had seen the ghost, and *spoken* to the ghost. And old Dugal kept right on saying that till the day they found him sleeping peacefully in the heather and the life all run out of him." He cupped his rough brown hand and tapped the ashes from his pipe. "Sixty years ago, it was, Angus. On a day like this. A long time."

"A long time," agreed Angus. He frowned. "And nobody will have seen the ghost since then?"

"Nobody. Or at least if anybody had seen it he kept his mouth shut." Uncle Wull tossed a few more logs on the fire. "Anyway it's a good tale, is it no, for a wild night?"

"It is that," agreed Angus. It was wonderful, this feeling that was in him of knowing fear and safety both at the same time. He sat very still letting his body savor the full sweetness of it. A good tale for a wild night it had been all right. Only that and nothing more. For who believed in ghosts today? It was strange, though, how just *talking* about them made the skin tighten and grow cold on one's neck. Strange how the thin voice of an old man named Dugal Comrie could echo across sixty years of time. An old man who believed he had seen the ghost of Craigie Castle. An old man who had been found dead in the heather *still* believing it. . . .

In his big leather chair Uncle Wull sat and stared into the fireplace. His eyes, moist with the moistness of old age, followed the rise and fall of the yellow and blue and orange flames. Something he saw in them must have pleased him, for he smiled and nodded his head. The light from the fireplace gentled the deep lines on his Scottish face with its high cheek bones. His head bent forward slightly. His breathing went soft and regular. He slept.

Angus got up quietly from his chair and crossed to the window. The blackness outside was the blackness of the grave. It lay thick against the window pane, endlessly deep and high and wide. He stared out into the vast nothingness. Out there was Dunnach Moor. And in Dunnach Moor was a great crumbling pile of stone. Craigie Castle.

Suddenly the blackness outside the window was shattered with a brilliant flash of light. Angus felt his breath leave his body as Dunnach Moor, lonely and desolate in the distance, leaped into brightness. For one fierce, white instant he almost believed he could see the far-off towers of Craigie Castle. Then, with the blackness, came an enormous crash of thunder overhead.

Only in his mind did something of the brightness linger, a small kindle of fire as the idea dawned. It sputtered for an instant before bursting into flame. A clear, pure flame that lit up his mind as brightly as the lightning had lit up Dunnach Moor.

Tomorrow he would go to Craigie Castle.

Chapter Two

Old men's tales are one thing when told in the night, when the wind is on the prowl and windows tremble, and shadows crawl like dark spiders over panelled walls. They are something else again when the sun is a familiar redness in the sky; when the shadows are all gone and the flames are only ashes in a cold grate.

"And was I no the daft one last night!" Angus exclaimed angrily to himself after breakfast. "Why now should I be thinking at all of going all the way out to Craigie Castle? To see a ghost?" He grunted. "Och,

7

and it's fair stupid I'm getting even to think of it."

With Uncle Wull off to the herring fishing and school out for the summer, Angus settled down to his chores. He weeded in the little vegetable garden at the back of their cottage. He whistled as his fingers dug into the moist earth and tossed the weeds into the basket. He would forget this whole crazy business of Craigie Castle. Ghosts indeed!

Yet three times he caught himself, one knee resting on the ground, staring off into the distance. Always he had been looking at the same spot. Far up Dunnach Moor at where he knew was the great crumbling pile of stone that was Craigie Castle.

Each time he had shaken his head angrily as though to dislodge the thought that still clung to the edge of his mind. Each time he whistled a little louder as though to drum out the small, thin voice within him that kept whispering, *"It's feared ye are, Angus Campbell. It's feared ye are."*

Suddenly he stood up. He no longer whistled. He could feel the slow, measured beating of his heart under his woolen jersey. Daft it might be, but daft or no, there was no choice left for him at all. Not if he had to keep his respect for himself, and respect for yourself was no little thing if your name was Angus Campbell.

His mind made up, he turned and walked firmly

away, across the winding, dirt road leading down to the village of Aberdour. His feet at last in the tough grass and the tougher heather, he headed up the desolate moor—towards Craigie Castle.

He had been tempted at first to ask Davie Thomson to come along. Davie was the butcher's son and his best friend in Aberdour. Yet to ask Davie would have been to show fear. No, it would be better not to ask Davie. Not if he wanted to prove something to himself.

Surely in all of Scotland there was no lonelier place than Dunnach Moor. A wasteland of rocks and heather, it lay like a great stagnant pool of death as far as the eye could see. No wild flowers bloomed in Dunnach Moor. No trees grew there. No birds sang. Even Dunnach Loch in the center of the moor, was unable to lift the pale of gloom and bleakness. Its waters were too dark. Too deep. Too still.

Angus quickened his step. He wasn't afraid. Not really. Still, it was best to get past the black waters of Dunnach Loch; best to do what had to be done and do it quickly.

He could see the huge pile of crumbling rock now in the distance. He did not have to be told what it was. Craigie Castle. Larger it loomed and ever larger. He could see, while still some distance away, the ivy that coiled around the single tower like a great green ser-

pent. Above and to the right and left of the main entrance were two square gaps in the wall. Once these had been windows. Glassless now, they stared out unblinkingly at the desolate moor like two sightless eyes.

In spite of himself Angus felt his pace slacken. He could sense a coldness across his shoulders, although there was no chill in the air. His feet seemed to drag across the tangle of purple heather. There was something foreboding about the grim ruins of Craigie Castle. The larger grew the castle before him, the larger grew the fear within him.

He had almost come to a standstill when he heard the voice:

"Welcome to Craigie Castle, laddie."

Chapter Three

Angus felt his blood turn to ice. In all his life he had never been so frightened. With an effort he turned around, not quite knowing what to expect and ready for the worst. The sigh of relief that fell from his lips when he saw the speaker must have been heard half way across Dunnach Moor.

The speaker was a little man. A *very* little man. He wore a kilt of a tartan Angus had never seen before. A bright Balmoral tam was perched at a jaunty angle on his head. It was hard to say how old he was. He had an odd face that seemed one half smiles and one half wrinkles. His eyes were the bluest Angus had ever seen, and the merriest. He might have been a fairly young man who looked old. Or again he might have been a fairly old man who looked young.

"Och, and it's the grand fright ye gave me," said Angus. "It was myself was no expecting at all to meet anybody in the middle of Dunnach Moor."

"No more than I," said the little man. He didn't speak the words exactly as anyone in Aberdour would speak them, yet he spoke them like a native just the same. A *very* odd little man!

"Then it's sorry I am I frightened ye," said Angus. "I was only here to—" he stopped and could have bitten off his tongue. He felt the blood rise to his face.

The little man waited patiently. Then, when Angus didn't go on, he said, "To what, lad?"

Angus gulped. It was too late now. Och, and wouldn't he look like the daft one indeed when he admitted *why* he had come to Craigie Castle! He said, in a low voice, his eyes fixed on the ground, "I came to see if there really was a ghost in Craigie Castle."

The little man gasped in astonishment. "A *what?*"

Angus swallowed. He had *never* felt so foolish! "A ghost," he whispered.

"A ghost?" All of a sudden the little man started to shake with laughter. He didn't laugh just in his throat. Oh no. All of him joined in! He laughed from the bottom of his silver-buckled shoes to the red *toorie* on top of his Balmoral tam. He laughed and he laughed until the tears started to stream from his bright blue eyes.

The longer he laughed the redder Angus became. Finally, his cheeks on fire, he glowered back at the other. "It's a rare joke ye seem to find it," he said.

The little man wiped his eyes. "Och, and why not, lad? A ghost? Today? Why *nobody* believes in ghosts any more." He chuckled again and fixed his blue eyes on the boy. "What will be your name, lad?"

"Angus."

"Angus?" The stranger seemed pleased. "A grand name that. A grand Scottish name."

"Aye, it is that," acknowledged Angus proudly. "What's more, I'm a Campbell."

"Fancy that now! Angus Campbell, eh?"

"Himself."

"A proud name. A *very* proud name."

Angus felt his chest rise. "Aye. It's no everyone that will be having it." He suddenly stared at the other. "Ye will no be having it yourself now, will ye?"

The little man shook his head. "It's another name I have. One no less proud, though, than yours." Suddenly he reached up and doffed his Balmoral. At the same moment he bent forward from the waist and swept the cap almost to the ground before him. "Mr. Mac-

Spurtle!" he cried gallantly, "and at your service, Angus Campbell."

At any other time Angus would have laughed had anyone struck such a pose. He didn't laugh now. Somehow he sensed something of the true chivalry behind Mr. MacSpurtle's action—a chivalry that long ago was a commonplace thing in the Highlands. He pulled his shoulders back, tilted his head, and said, "It's honored I am to meet ye, Mr. MacSpurtle."

"And ye also, Angus Campbell."

"MacSpurtle," mused Angus. "There will no be many in these parts with the name."

The little man shook his head ruefully. "In these parts or in other parts. When ye come to think about it, ye *seldom* meet a MacSpurtle today."

Angus nodded. It was quite true. Most people you meet are non-MacSpurtles.

The stranger sighed. "Aye, but once it was different. Once this moor rang with the shouts of the Mac-Spurtles." A strange, fierce light gleamed deep in the blue eyes. He looked away into the emptiness of the moor as though seeing something there, something that caused his chin to set in a firm, proud line. "This land was MacSpurtle land! The glens MacSpurtle glens. The lochs MacSpurtle lochs. The sound of our pipes crashed and echoed in the hills. The ground trembled beneath the feet of our fighting men." He stopped. Slowly the light went dim in his eyes. Slowly the firmness slid from the square jaw. He was no longer the proud chieftain glorying in the might of his clan. He was a tired little man gazing at an empty moor.

Uncle Wull had always told Angus that if at any time he didn't know what to say, he should say nothing. Angus at that moment didn't know what to say, so great was the pity in his heart. Wisely he said nothing. In a few seconds Mr. MacSpurtle was his old self again. His face was wreathed in broad smiles.

"Och now, and why talk such foolishness? And to a wee laddie at that! Let the dead bury their dead say I." He smiled with sly good humor at the boy. "After all, now, how could the dead bury their dead?" He chuckled.

Angus, catching the note of banter, reddened again. "It's well ye know, Mr. MacSpurtle, I don't believe in ghosts."

"Aye, but ye came out here to find one just the same."

"I came out here to *prove* there wasn't one at all." He scoffed. "The Ghost of Craigie Castle indeed!"

Mr. MacSpurtle raised his eyebrows gently. "And how will ye prove it, Angus?"

Angus frowned. "Prove what, Mr. MacSpurtle?"

"That there's no Ghost of Craigie Castle."

Angus hesitated. Of course there was only one thing

to do. The thing he had come to do in the first place, which was to go into Craigie Castle. Still he had rather *hoped* that Mr. MacSpurtle wouldn't have brought the matter up. Ghost or no ghost there was something menacing about Craigie Castle; something sinister in its very stillness; in the way it lay athwart the moor like a great beast, crouched and tensed to spring.

He said loudly in a voice befitting a Campbell. "Prove it? Why, by going into Craigie Castle! And why no?"

The little man in the kilt smiled. "Ye will no be minding, will ye, if I go along with ye?" he asked.

Together they walked through the yawning gap in the wall that was the door of Craigie Castle.

Chapter Four

Despite the presence of Mr. Mac-Spurtle alongside of him, Angus could hear the hammering of his heart loud in his ears. It was daft. What was there to be afraid of? If Mr. MacSpurtle ever suspected how frightened he was, the little man would split his sides laughing.

Together they scrambled over the debris scattered in the narrow courtyard inside the walls. It was plain to see that this had been used when the castle was under attack. Beyond the courtyard loomed a door more massive than the one through which they had just entered. Like the other it was hardly a door any more, though. Only a great arch sagging with ivy and a heap of smooth time-worn stones beneath.

In spite of the fear within him, Angus could still marvel at the sure-footed way that Mr. MacSpurtle crossed the mounds of fallen stone. The little man was as light-footed as a mountain goat. He also seemed to have an uncanny skill in knowing *exactly* where to step —or where not to step. Once, faced by a sudden, sharp drop, he coolly leaped across the chasm, his quick feet somehow finding the one firm rock on the other side of the steep drop. Angus, his blood jolting a little too fast through his veins, made the leap too, although hardly so gracefully. Scrambling to his feet, he followed Mr. MacSpurtle into the great central hall of Craigie Castle.

The light seeping in through the gaps in the walls and roof revealed a scene of decay and ruin. Rocks and stones, cemented with weeds, were scattered every- where. Strangely enough the huge fireplace still stood at the far end of the hall. The towering walls too, had largely escaped the assaults of time and war. They stood, blackened by fire and weary with age. Their shadows crawled over the debris for all the world like a thick, dark undergrowth.

It was the stillness Angus noticed most of all. It seemed to press in from every side. The only sound

was the sound of their breathing. Once, from high in
the eaves, a bird suddenly twittered. Its small, thin
voice echoed mournfully through the great empty hall.
Then the stillness was there again, a stillness even
more massive than before.

"No one seems to be home," murmured Mr. Mac-
Spurtle.

Angus nodded quick agreement. This might be a
good time to get out. "Aye, it's plain to see, is it no,
that there's no ghost here."

Mr. MacSpurtle frowned. "Maybe it's a little deaf,
he is. He must be an *old* ghost. Maybe I'd better call
him."

Angus looked around uneasily. It was one thing to
go looking for a ghost. It was something else again to
go *hunting* for one. Which was what Mr. MacSpurtle
seemed about to do. Still he couldn't very well say no
to the idea. Not after the little man had laughed so
heartily at him. Remembering Uncle Wull's advice to
say nothing at such times, he kept his mouth shut.

Mr. MacSpurtle, though, hadn't heard of Uncle
Wull. It was only natural therefore, that he hadn't
heard of Uncle Wull's advice. Anyway, unlike Angus,
he opened his mouth. Wide. The stillness within the
castle was shattered into a thousand pieces. Angus almost jumped out of his shoes as Mr. MacSpurtle's
wild *Hullooo-ooo* broke from his lips. It was loud

enough to wake the dead, a thought that didn't help Angus's peace of mind.

The echoes washed back eerily from the walls. Small, shocked voices protested from every corner of the great hall. Finally the last thin, hushed, reedy voice faded away. Silence settled on Craigie Castle like snow on the waters of Dunnach Loch.

Mr. MacSpurtle frowned. "Shall I try again?" he asked. He *almost* looked disappointed. "Maybe he's *very* deaf."

"No!" said Angus firmly. Uncle Wull or no Uncle Wull there were times you *had* to open your mouth.

The little man chuckled. "Then it's satisfied ye are that there's no ghost in Craigie Castle?"

"Aye," said Angus fervently. "I was satisfied before. But it's more than satisfied I am now. I'm *sure.*"

"That's good Scottish logic," Mr. MacSpurtle said approvingly. He looked around. He *still* seemed a little disappointed. "Ah well," he said reluctantly, "maybe it would be more good Scottish logic if we got out of here. Ye have a long way home if I'm no mistaken."

Quite clearly this was another time when it was better to say something than to say nothing. Angus said in a clear, ringing voice, "A grand idea."

Mr. MacSpurtle took one last, hopeful look around. Finally, with a sigh, he set his Balmoral firmly on his head. Next, he straightened the sporran on his kilt.

Then, with a light skip he was on top of a fallen pillar, Angus on his heels. Together they passed through the large arch and into the courtyard.

It was only when they had passed through the second crumbling door that the thought came back to Angus. The thought that had been squirming around on the edges of his mind all afternoon.

He stopped suddenly. He stared at the stranger.

"And what brought ye to Craigie Castle this day, Mr. MacSpurtle?"

Chapter Five

Mr. MacSpurtle cocked his head to the side like a bird. His bright eyes regarded the boy. He said mildly, "Ye forget, Angus, I am a MacSpurtle. This castle belonged to the MacSpurtles. Ye might say this is our home."

Angus nodded, not quite sure he understood. One thing was certain, though. Mr. MacSpurtle must have visited the castle often. That would explain his sureness of foot when he picked his way through the rubble.

"So ye might say ye own this castle?"

"Ye might at that."

Angus smiled. There was something comical about the idea of Mr. MacSpurtle owning a castle, even one like this. He said jokingly, "Och now, and what if some of the other MacSpurtles come and claim the castle?"

"There *are* no other MacSpurtles," said the little man sorrowfully. "Ye see before ye, Angus Campbell, the last of the great clan MacSpurtle." He sighed. "I have been the last for a long time. A long, long time."

It was odd, thought Angus, staring at him. He doesn't *look* old. Not really. Surely not as old as Uncle Wull who was *very* old. Mr. MacSpurtle now, why, his hair was a light brown! Of course, he's got wrinkles but then *all* grown-ups have wrinkles. You couldn't be a grown-up *without* wrinkles. Besides, look at the way Mr. MacSpurtle had skipped around inside the castle! What old man could possibly have done that? Och, and it was daft just to think about it!

For some reason Mr. MacSpurtle looked very sad. All of the gentle good humor was gone from his face. Perhaps he was remembering all of the other Mac-Spurtles, thought Angus. Or maybe just the fact that he wasn't as young as he once was. That must be it, he reasoned. To cheer the little man he said, "Och now, and it's no so old ye are yourself, Mr. MacSpurtle. No half as old as Uncle Wull."

"Uncle Wull? And who might Uncle Wull be?"

"Uncle Wull Campbell. *My* great-uncle. We live together, Uncle Wull and myself. It was Uncle Wull who told me all about old Dugal Comrie."

"Dugal Comrie?" Mr. MacSpurtle frowned. He tugged thoughtfully at his long lower lip. "Dugal Comrie. H-m-m. Seems to me I knew a Dugal Comrie once."

Angus laughed. "Aye, but ye never knew *this* Dugal Comrie." It tickled him to put something over on the little man. "This Dugal Comrie said he had seen the Ghost of Craigie Castle. Old Dugal has been dead for sixty years."

"*That* long?" murmured Mr. MacSpurtle absently.

It was an odd remark. Angus hesitated a moment before he went on.

"Aye, old Dugal died still claiming he had seen the ghost." Angus shook his head sympathetically. "Poor old man."

"He was a young man once," said Mr. MacSpurtle mildly. "Ye might say that an old man is really only a young man who's been around longer."

Angus nodded uncertainly. It was hard to understand Mr. MacSpurtle sometimes.

"Aye, but an old man knows more," he said, determined to get the last word in. "Like Uncle Wull," he added proudly.

"An old man *remembers* more, Angus Campbell. There's a difference, lad." He paused, then said in a very soft voice, "For example, an old man might remember when there were trees in this part of Dunnach Moor. Many trees. Then came the great fire sweeping down from the hills. Aye, and it's himself might remember further back than that. To when Bonnie Prince Charlie stole across this very moor with six picked men. That would be during the rebellion of 1745."

Angus stared. "But Mr. MacSpurtle, it's daft the old man would have been for certain! *Everybody* knows the Prince was never in Dunnach Moor."

Mr. MacSpurtle said gently, "I'm no talking about knowing. I'm talking about *remembering*. And this same old man would remember too when the Prince, on his horse, forded the stream that ran into Dunnach Loch. Up by Cameron's Mill it was where the water ran shallow."

Angus felt his mind go dizzy. "Mr. MacSpurtle! Mr. MacSpurtle! It's well ye know there's *no* stream goes into Dunnach Loch. And there's *no* mill called Cameron's Mill!"

Mr. MacSpurtle shook his head. "There was a stream *then*. *And* a mill called Cameron's Mill."

"But why should the Prince come to Dunnach Moor at all?" cried Angus.

"He came, Angus, to enlist the help of the Mac-Spurtles of Craigie Castle in his bid for the throne of England and Scotland. Aye, right here to Craigie Castle came Charlie himself."

"And why did he come with only six men, him being the Prince?"

"Because, Angus, he came by night and in secret. The MacSpurtles had not rallied to the Prince when he landed from France and raised his banner in the Hebrides. He dared not, at that moment, openly seek the MacSpurtle help. For Angus, had he done so, all Scotland would have known. And had the MacSpurtles refused, other clans might have followed their lead."

Angus nodded. It made sense. If *anything* made sense any more.

"So he came by night, the Prince and the six trusted followers. He rode on a black horse with a black cape around him. It was on the night of August tenth. There was no moon in the sky. It was strangely cold for an August night. Low on his black horse, his cape streaming in the wind behind him, the Prince swept across Dunnach Moor. When he left Craigie Castle he had received the pledge of the MacSpurtles to stand with him." He paused. "That was why it was, Angus, that no one knew at all that he came here. Only the Mac-Spurtles knew. And few there were of them to tell the story after the clans were crushed at the Battle of Culloden."

Mr. MacSpurtle stopped and shook his head. Finally, he sighed and after a moment smiled again. "Well, that's what I mean, Angus Campbell. Nobody *knows* that. But an old man might *remember* it just the same, eh?"

"Aye," said Angus, "but it's forgetting one thing ye are."

"And what might that be?"

"The old man would have to be more than two hundred years old."

Again Mr. MacSpurtle smiled. "That's right, Angus, he would." He put his hand in the sporran of his kilt and took out a silver coin. "Here's something for ye, laddie. For sweeties!"

"Och, and I would no—"

"Weesh! All laddies like sweeties. And your Uncle Wull will be wondering what's happened to ye." He put out his hand. "A good journey home."

Angus took his hand in his. "And a good journey home to yourself, Mr. MacSpurtle," he said earnestly. All at once he realized how fond he had grown of this queer little man with the strange tales.

When he had gone about thirty yards he turned and waved back. Mr. MacSpurtle was standing, one foot on a boulder, looking after him. His kilt and the black ribbons at the back of his Balmoral moved gently in the breeze. He raised his right arm and waved back at the boy. His voice, blunted by the wind, carried to Angus's ears:

"A good journey home, Angus Campbell."

It was a few moments later that Angus came to a dead stop in the heather. He had clean forgotten to ask Mr. MacSpurtle where *his* home was!

He wheeled around. Mr. MacSpurtle was gone. Puzzled, Angus stared across the flat bleakness of Dunnach Moor. Nothing moved. Nothing stirred. Anywhere.

It was impossible! There was no place where a man could be hidden from view on Dunnach Moor! No place at all except in Craigie Castle. And why should Mr. MacSpurtle think of going in *there* again?

Angus stared across the nakedness of the great moor. Nothing moved. Nothing stirred. Anywhere.

Chapter Six

It was all very strange. Angus's mind was an overturned beehive of buzzing, stinging thoughts. What had Mr. MacSpurtle been doing in the wilds of Dunnach Moor? He had never really said. And where had he gone to? It could only have been the castle. Yet why should he go *there*?

And hadn't it been odd that he should have known a Dugal Comrie once? It wasn't a common name. *"That long,"* he had muttered when Angus had told him Dugal had been dead for sixty years. Almost as though it had been the *same* Dugal Comrie....

There were other things, too. The peculiar way he spoke, almost like a native yet not quite. And his kilt with its odd tartan. No doubt it was the ancient Mac-Spurtle tartan. Where had Mr. MacSpurtle been able to get such a kilt, though? Surely there hadn't been any around for a long time.

Yet more than anything else Angus's thoughts kept turning to Bonnie Prince Charlie. What did it all mean? *"An old man might remember,"* Mr. Mac-Spurtle had said. How could *any* man remember something that had happened more than two hundred years ago? It was daft! Still, Mr. MacSpurtle hadn't *seemed* daft. In fact, he had seemed very alert.

On an impulse, Angus stopped before the cottage of Jamie Grant, the schoolmaster. Mr. Grant, in addition to being the local authority on the history of Aberdour, was one of his best friends. He was a man of medium size, with gray eyes and short, sandy hair. Always, when Angus called on him, there was a plate of buttered oatcakes on the table. There was a plate there now and Mr. Grant waved his hand toward them.

"Eat up, Angus. Oatcakes were made for boys. Or perhaps boys were made for oatcakes." He smiled and the skin creased around his eyes. "I'm never sure which way it is."

"Thank ye kindly, Mr. Grant," said Angus. He was hungry. He hadn't eaten since breakfast. It was strange, though, how the rich, nutty flavor of the oatcake in his mouth didn't excite him at all. He munched absently, his mind a million miles away. Suddenly his jaws went still. He said, "Mr. Grant, was there a moon on the night of August 10, 1745?"

The schoolmaster, on the point of pouring hot water for tea into the pot, almost scalded himself.

"Eh?"

"And was it a cold night besides?"

Mr. Grant put the hot water down carefully before answering. "I'm sure I don't know, Angus," he said. "Somehow the subject never came up before." He smiled with his gray eyes.

"But I've *got* to know, Mr. Grant! I've just *got* to."

Startled at the earnestness in the boy's voice, the schoolmaster looked at him doubtfully. "Well, if it's *that* important I imagine I could look up the old records. If there had been a frost or such that night it might have affected the crops. As for the moon—" He shrugged. "Anything else you want me to look up while I'm at it?" he asked good-naturedly.

Angus nodded his head promptly. "Aye, Mr. Grant, there is, and it's glad I am ye brought the matter up and no myself."

"But—

"There will be the matter, Mr. Grant, of the stream that ran into Dunnach Loch."

"What stream, Angus? Dunnach Loch is fed by deep springs. There's no streams running—"

"Och, and I mean the one by Cameron's Mill."

The schoolmaster looked at him in bewilderment. "Cameron's Mill? But there's no mill—"

"It was shallow there, Mr. Grant," explained Angus patiently. "That was why Bonnie Prince Charlie crossed there."

The schoolmaster said weakly, "Crossed there?"

"Aye, when he was riding over Dunnach Moor that night."

Mr. Grant held up his hands. Then he placed them tenderly one on each side of his head. He sighed. "Angus. Angus. *Please* go a little more slowly." He closed his eyes for almost ten seconds. He sighed again. "Now then. What is all this about Bonnie Prince Charlie crossing Dunnach Moor? Surely you know from the history I've been teaching you that Bonnie Prince Charlie *never* was near Dunnach Moor, far less crossing it. It's in all the history books."

"But don't ye see, Mr. Grant, history books or no, he *had* to cross Dunnach Moor! For, if he didn't, how could he get to Craigie Castle?"

The schoolmaster said, a little grimly, "And why should he want to go to Craigie Castle?"

"To get the help of the MacSpurtles, that's why, Mr. Grant."

"I see," said the schoolmaster, the slight edge of grimness still in his voice. "And why should he go there at night?"

"I'm no saying he really *went* there at night, Mr. Grant. But if he *had* to go to the castle, then he *had* to go at night. If he had gone in the daytime all Scotland would have known about it. And if the MacSpurtles had refused to go out with him all Scotland would have known that too. It would have been a terrible blow to Charlie, would it no, and him just over from France."

"H-m-m." The schoolmaster was looking at the boy curiously. "H-m-m," he said again. He seemed to be doing a lot of thinking.

"Ye see, Mr. Grant, that's why the Prince would have had to come at night. That's why there had to be no moon at all. That's why too he chose a cold night when the crofters would be home by their fires. The fewer that saw Charlie that night, the better."

Mr. Grant's shrewd gray eyes never left the boy. "H-m-m," he said again. He said it a little louder this time, as though he had come to a decision. Finally, with a sigh he crossed over to his window. For a long moment he stared out at the loneliest place in all Scotland—Dunnach Moor. "I don't know what this is all about," he said at last. "It sounds mad and yet—" He shrugged. "I'll do what I can to help you. It may take some days, though."

"Thank ye, Mr. Grant," Angus said gratefully as he made his way to the door, "thank ye kindly."

"Don't mention it," the schoolmaster said. He added a little drily, "In fact I'd rather you didn't. The tax-payers in Aberdour would think they had a daft school-teacher on their hands. Goodby, Angus."

"Goodby, Mr. Grant, and thank ye for the oatcakes! They were that grand."

"Bonnie Prince Charlie," Angus heard the school-master mutter as he closed the door, "could it be possible—? NO!"

The violence with which Mr. Grant slammed the heavy door shut caused the iron knocker to fall with a dull dour *clunk*.

Chapter Seven

There was a queer look in the eyes of Jamie Grant, schoolmaster of Aberdour, when he met Angus four days later. Angus, who had just come out of Gowrie's Bakery on High Street with a bag of warm rolls, fairly rushed across the street to greet him.

"Mr. Grant! Mr. Grant! Did ye find out anything?" he asked.

"I did, Angus."

The boy felt his heart skip a beat. He did not trust the words his seething mind forced on his lips. He stood quite still. For some reason he couldn't understand there was a strange lightness in his legs.

Mr. Grant said slowly, "I have checked all of the old records I could find. I have even been in touch with authorities in Glasgow and Edinburgh." He paused.

Angus wet his lips. Wouldn't the man *ever* get to it!

"There was no moon on the night of August 10, 1745."

Angus waited, breathless.

"There was frost on the ground."

Angus nodded. His lips were dry. Drier than they had ever been.

"Two hundred years ago a man named Cameron had a mill." Again Mr. Grant paused. "It was on a stream long since dried up. The stream ran into Dunnach Loch. The stream was usually crossed at Cameron's Mill."

"Ah!" It was not so much an exclamation as a sigh. It seemed to rise all the way from Angus's heart to his lips.

The schoolmaster continued quietly. "Whether Prince Charlie crossed that stream no one knows. But we do know that on the night of August tenth he and six of his chieftans were missing from camp."

Angus stood very still. He could feel his nails dig deep into his hands.

"What happened that night we do not know, either. But what we do know is that on the morning of August eleventh, the MacSpurtles of Craigie Castle came out for the Prince."

Angus stood quite still, a bag of rolls in his hand, a wonder in his heart.

Mr. Grant said softly, when Angus did not speak, "How did you know these things, Angus?" His gray eyes stared curiously at the boy.

"Och, Mr. Grant and it's no a question at all of *knowing*. It's a question of remembering—" He stopped. He could feel his face grow warm.

"Remembering?" Mr. Grant frowned. "How do you remember something that happened more than two hundred years ago?"

"I—" Angus began. He swallowed hard. He knew his face was a fiery red. Yet he couldn't tell Mr. Grant about Mr. MacSpurtle. Not yet. Not until he knew a little more. Yet his friend *deserved* to know.

"Would ye mind at all, Mr. Grant, if I told ye next week?" he asked anxiously. Another week should give him a lot of answers to a lot of questions.

"Next week? Very well, Angus." The schoolmaster smiled slightly. "After all, what's a week compared to two hundred years? Goodby, Angus."

"Goodby, Mr. Grant!" cried Angus. "And thank ye kindly for all your bother!"

The ancient *wag o' the wall* clock in the kitchen was striking nine when Angus rushed in with the rolls.

It was *still* striking nine when he rushed out again.

Chapter Eight

H*ow had Mr. MacSpurtle known?*

Again and again that question stabbed into Angus's mind as he crossed Dunnach Moor. No one, not even his friend Mr. Grant, who knew *everything*, had known what Mr. MacSpurtle had known. How had *he* known?

There were other questions too. What had Mr. Mac-Spurtle meant when he had talked about an old man remembering these things? No man, no matter how old, could remember something that happened more than two hundred years ago. Yet Mr. MacSpurtle had said it very clearly. *An old man might remember....*

Och, and there were *many* questions to be answered.

40

And only one man could do the answering of them! A little man with a queer tongue in him and bright blue eyes. A little man who wore the kilt of a vanished clan. A little man named Mr. MacSpurtle.

Now he was midway across the moor. Had it been over this dreary waste of rocks and heather that Bonnie Prince Charlie had ridden that moonless night so long ago? In a way it was hard to believe. The Stuart prince had loved life. This was a place of death. The Prince had loved brightness. Dunnach Moor was desolation. The Prince had loved song and laughter. Here was the stillness of the grave.

Slowly, as he drew nearer to Craigie Castle, Angus felt the first stirring of something like fear within him. Thinking things out in the safety of Aberdour was one thing. Thinking them out in the middle of Dunnach Moor was something else again.

Why had he come here at all? Was it *so* important that he learn more about Mr. MacSpurtle? Besides, the whole thing was foolish. Why should he expect that Mr. MacSpurtle would be anywhere near Craigie Castle? Better turn around and go home. No one had seen him go. Most likely no one would see him return.

He hesitated for a long moment. To go back now was to face Mr. Grant again. What could he possibly tell his good friend? That he had been told the stories about Bonnie Prince Charlie by a little man. A little man he had been *afraid* to see again? No, he couldn't do that. That was one of the sorrows of having a proud name like Angus Campbell. People expected you to act in the manner of the great heroes of clan Campbell. You *had* to do things that other people with other names didn't. Angus sighed. There was no way out of it. As a Campbell he *had* to go on.

The weather had turned bad. A damp wind leaned flatly across the moor. Dark clouds hung limp in the sky, too loggy with rain to move. In the strange half light the heather glowed dully like spilt, dark blood. A whaup, far from home, suddenly passed, trailing its long mournful cry behind it. The eerie sound of the curlew, in the stillness of the moor, made Angus jump.

Craigie Castle lay just ahead of him now. In the pale light it seemed even larger than before. Larger and more terrifying.

He walked very slowly. He could feel the tug of the heather against his feet, almost as though it was begging him to stay where he was. To go no further.

Angus was still fifty yards away when he saw him. He was standing just inside the gate of the castle. He had on his kilt. His Balmoral was cocked jauntily on his head. He didn't seem surprised to see the boy. He waved Angus to a flat stone as a host would offer a chair to a guest. He smiled.

"Welcome again to Craigie Castle, Angus Campbell. And make yourself at home!"

Chapter Nine

I have come here, Mr. MacSpurtle, to ask ye a few questions," Angus said in a low voice. He stood a safe distance away. He pretended not to see the seat that Mr. MacSpurtle had offered.

"The best way to get an answer is to ask a question," said Mr. MacSpurtle. His blue eyes were so friendly and his smile so warm that Angus was emboldened to come a little closer. As he drew nearer, he suddenly noticed the bagpipe propped against a rock. The idea of Mr. MacSpurtle with his skinny little frame puffing away at the pipes made Angus smile inwardly. Again he drew closer.

"A fine day, is it no, Angus?" asked Mr. MacSpurtle agreeably. He screwed up his face and cocked a blue eye at the dark, dreary sky. "Och, no sun to be sure. Still, who will be needing sun all the time now? It's the peace and quiet, lad. Aye, these are the things that matter. Peace and quiet. Listen!" Mr. MacSpurtle bent his head. "Do ye hear anything?"

Angus listened. Not a sound carried to his ears. He shook his head.

Mr. MacSpurtle beamed. *"That's* what I mean, Angus! Peace and quiet. And there's no place in all Scotland like Dunnach Moor for the peace and quiet!"

"Aye," Angus said. There was no question about *that.*

"I'll tell ye something," Mr. MacSpurtle said. "I come of a fighting clan as well ye know. Och, and it was the bonnie fighters were the MacSpurtles. But no me. I'm a man of peace and quiet. That's why I love Dunnach Moor." He smiled. "Ye might say, Angus, it's as quiet as a tomb."

"Ye might at that," Angus replied. He wished Mr. MacSpurtle wouldn't talk about things like tombs. Not in Craigie Castle.

"Ye came to ask a few questions," Mr. MacSpurtle reminded him.

"Aye, I did." Now that he had to ask them he found it difficult to say them. He stood awkwardly. He shifted his weight from foot to foot. Mr. MacSpurtle regarded him mildly. Suddenly, like a dam bursting, the words spilled out.

"How did ye know, Mr. MacSpurtle, about Cameron's Mill and the stream running into Dunnach Moor? Nobody in all Aberdour was knowing these things. Aye, no even Mr. Grant, the schoolmaster. And how could ye have known about Bonnie Prince Charlie? Aye, and the fact that there was no moon at all and the frost on the ground? How did ye know these things, Mr. MacSpurtle, and no other man knowing them?"

His strength suddenly spent with the words, Angus stood waiting. The beating of his heart was the loudest sound in all Dunnach Moor.

Mr. MacSpurtle said gently, "Perhaps, Angus, the reason that no other man knew these things is because I am no the same as other men."

"Aye, and ye knew Dugal Comrie too," whispered Angus.

Mr. MacSpurtle moved his slight shoulders in a shrug. "Many men knew Dugal. So did I."

"But Dugal died a long time ago. Aye, and so did the men who knew him." Angus's breath was a lump in his throat. "But ye didn't."

Mr. MacSpurtle sighed. "That will be a matter of opinion, Angus Campbell."

They stood quite still. Mr. MacSpurtle and Angus Campbell. The man with the gentle smile. The boy with the frightened eyes. The words so quickly spoken still trembled in the air.

Angus opened his mouth. No cry came out. He wanted to run but his legs were rooted to the ground. Fear, like no fear he had ever known, had him in its grip.

"Don't be frightened, Angus," said Mr. MacSpurtle, "it is no becoming to a Campbell."

The words that Angus spoke when he spoke them were hardly words at all. Only a trembling movement of his frozen lips.

"Who will ye be?"

"The Ghost of Craigie Castle," said Mr. MacSpurtle.

Chapter Ten

"Och, now, and don't be surprised at all," chided Mr. MacSpurtle. "After all, did ye no come to Craigie Castle to look for a ghost? Why should ye be surprised then to find one?"

"A ghost?" whispered Angus. It was unreal. This couldn't be happening to him. But it was. Mr. MacSpurtle had seated himself, as large as life, on a flat stone. His lips were puckered in a dry whistle.

"A ghost," agreed Mr. MacSpurtle.

Like one in a trance Angus muttered, "But ghosts wear white robes—"

"All except MacSpurtle ghosts! *They* wear the kilt! Och, now, and can ye imagine a Highlander wrapped up in a white sheet?" Mr. MacSpurtle shuddered. "It's no the right length, besides."

"—and chains—"

"Chains?" Mr. MacSpurtle smiled a little sadly. He shook his head. "Chains are for men. Chains of pride. Of greed. Of envy."

"—and they walk at night—"

"Only those who can't sleep," explained Mr. Mac-Spurtle promptly. "Ghosts are like people, Angus. When they find they can't sleep at night they walk around a bit. Of course, they go around moaning about it. It makes good Scottish sense to grumble when ye can't sleep. Am I no right, lad?"

It was strange how his fears were slowly dying away. Under the spell of Mr. MacSpurtle's good-natured voice Angus could feel his courage returning. "Aye," he said. He looked at the other. "Ye must be very old, Mr. MacSpurtle?"

"*Very* old, I'm fearing." The little ghost sighed. "And *very* tired. It's anxious I am to join the rest of the Mac-Spurtles and it's weary they are of waiting for me on the other side. Aye, it's tired I am for certain, and lonely at times. The last of the MacSpurtles." He shook his head mournfully.

"And what keeps ye here?"

"*This!*" With an exclamation of anger and grief Mr. MacSpurtle brought his hand down hard on his bagpipe. "Of all the evil things made by the hand of man, Angus Campbell, the bagpipe will be the worst."

Angus stared at him, shocked. Shocked that Mr. MacSpurtle, so mild-mannered and gentle, should show such fire. Shocked more, that anyone with a name like MacSpurtle should speak ill of the pipes.

"Mind ye," added Mr. MacSpurtle grudgingly, "I'm no saying they don't sound just grand. *If* ye can play them." He ran his fingers sadly over the drones and the chanter. "I can't."

"And why no?" Angus asked. "After all, it's all the time in the world ye have to practise."

"It's no time I need, Angus. It's breath."

"Breath?"

"Aye, I'm no built to play the pipes. Ye see this bag here? Well that's the part ye have to fill up with air before ye can squeeze out a wee tune." Mr. Mac-Spurtle's blue eyes swam with tears. "Look at the size of my chest, Angus. And look at the size of that bag. How could *anybody* like me breathe hard enough to fill *that* thing up with air?"

"But what will it be mattering, Mr. MacSpurtle? It's many people there are who can't play the pipes."

"Aye, but none of them be a MacSpurtle. Ye see, Angus, in our clan there is no such thing as a Mac-

Spurtle who can't play the pipes. That's why I'm still here. Until I squeeze a tune out of that thing there, it's myself is no worthy to join the MacSpurtles on the other side."

Angus said softly, "Then it's yourself has been trying for a long time, Mr. MacSpurtle?"

"A long time. Day after day. Year after year."

A thought suddenly came to Angus. He said, "That night Prince Charlie came were you—?"

Mr. MacSpurtle nodded. "Aye. I was on the moor with my pipes. Then all at once there he was on his black horse on his way to the castle. He galloped past, his black cloak flying in the wind." The saddest of smiles flitted across his face as he looked down at his bagpipe. "Of course he never heard me at all."

Fear had long since left Angus. There was only pity now, for poor Mr. MacSpurtle, for the tunes he could hear only in his heart.

"Ye must keep on trying, Mr. MacSpurtle," he urged. "Ye must keep on trying all the time. For if ye don't try ye will *never* get a tune out of them. Och, and why don't ye try right now?"

The little ghost brushed his hand roughly across his moist eyes. He blew his nose loudly. He picked up the pipes. "I'll try again, Angus," he said.

Slowly he put the blow pipe to his lips. He placed his fingers on the air holes. He took a deep—deep—

deep breath. His scrawny chest heaved until it strained against the pearl buttons on his velvet jacket. His cheeks grew round and red like two bright apples. His elbows flayed the tartan bag under his arm. He huffed and he puffed. He wheezed and he squeezed. Yet in spite of all his efforts not a single, solitary peep came out of his bagpipe. To Angus's ears the stillness of Dunnach Moor had never been as still as it was now that poor Mr. MacSpurtle tried to play his pipes.

Finally, Mr. MacSpurtle gave up. He took a silk handkerchief from his velvet jacket and dabbed his brow. "Ye see, Angus? I'll never get a tune out of it. Never! And if I never get a tune out of it, how will I ever be able to join the rest of the MacSpurtles?"

Angus tried not to look at Mr. MacSpurtle's face, small and tight with misery. He tried to think of something to say that would help. "At least ye have the peace and quiet of Dunnach Moor," he said helpfully.

"Aye, I've got that right enough," Mr. MacSpurtle said bitterly. "It will take more than my bagpipe playing to change it." He rubbed his finger in the corner of his eye. *The last of the MacSpurtles.*

The words were a heaviness in Angus's throat and he dared not speak them. Yet after all it was just as well. For what words could he speak that would help? If all of the words from all of the world were gathered up and brought to Dunnach Moor there would not be among all of them the words that would bring comfort to Mr. MacSpurtle.

The little ghost was still slumped forward, his head resting on his knees, when Angus tiptoed away.

Chapter Eleven

It took exactly six hours before everyone in the village had heard the news. The last person to get the story was old Malcolm Fraser. Malcolm was ninety-two and the oldest villager in Aberdour. He was also the deafest. Malcolm *always* got the news last. When old Malcolm cupped his hand to his ear and nodded, it always meant one thing. There was no one left in all the village of Aberdour who hadn't heard that particular story.

It had all been Angus's fault. Och, and he could have bitten off his tongue afterward! But how could any boy meet a ghost and not tell his best friend about it? It was too much to ask of anyone. And, of course, Davie Thomson, wide-eyed and excited, had promised to tell *nobody*. Still, you could hardly call one's father a *nobody* now, could you? Big Rab Thomson, the village butcher, had been equally wide-eyed and excited as he listened to his son. And Rab, to do him justice, hadn't told the story to the first person he met. After all, that would have been dour-faced Tam Lauder and Rab wasn't going to tell the likes of *him* first! Rab saved it for his friend, Jock Stewart. After all he *had* to tell Jock. For if he hadn't he would have been placing him in the same class as dour-faced Tam. What way was *that* to treat a friend? So Rab told Jock. And Jock told Geordie Clyde. Dour-faced Tam did get the story finally, just ahead of old Malcolm Fraser. When Malcolm cupped his hand to his ear and listened to Tam Lauder, exactly six hours had passed since Angus had whispered the story to Davie Thomson.

It was Mr. Peter Pettybone who had set off the reaction. As Secretary of the Town Council, Mr. Pettybone was a man of some importance in Aberdour. A man of narrow views, Mr. Pettybone talked a great deal. When a closed mind and an open mouth get together, trouble usually isn't too far away. Angus found out just how far away when he sat across the table from Uncle Wull that night. The old man had fidgeted with his broth all during the meal. Suddenly he had brought his spoon down hard and scowled at the boy.

"Angus, it is well ye should know this. They are talking about ye in the village."

"Aye, I know." *Why* hadn't he kept his mouth shut!

"It's about that ghost ye said ye saw."

"Aye."

Uncle Wull hesitated. "Mr. Pettybone says ye *didn't* see it."

"Eh?"

"Mr. Pettybone says ye didn't see it," his uncle repeated. "He says there's no such thing as a ghost. In Craigie Castle or any place. He reads a lot, does Mr. Pettybone, and he says science has *proved* what he says. Mr. Pettybone is a great man for science, aye, and a great talker besides."

"But Mr. MacSpurtle *is* a ghost! Why—"

"—and what's more, there's a lot of people in Aberdour believing him." He stopped and looked down at the table. His hands toyed with a crust of bread. He said flatly, "Those that believe *him*, Angus, will not be believing *you*."

Angus could hear the ticking of the clock, loud in his ears. He said miserably, "Ye believe me, Uncle Wull?"

"I believe *in* ye. And I know ye believe what ye say is true, or it's yourself would not be saying it." He paused. "But what will ye say to Mr. Pettybone?"

Angus stared. "And what can I say to the likes of him? It's a big man he is in Aberdour."

Uncle Wull said quietly, "Ye can say it's no lie ye tell. That's what ye can say to him."

Angus had never felt so miserable. For the hundredth time that day he could have wept for letting the story out in the first place. If only he had remembered Uncle Wull's advice to keep his mouth shut! *Now* look at the mess he was in. Never in all his life had he ever spoken to the Secretary of the Town Council. Now he was not only being asked to speak to him. He was being asked to correct him.

There was understanding in Uncle Wull's eyes. "Ye are a wee bit afraid to speak to the man?" he asked.

Angus nodded. "Aye, I am." He wet his lips. "But I'll speak to him just the same. For it's no lie I tell, Uncle Wull. There *is* a ghost in Craigie Castle."

Chapter Twelve

A ghost? In Craigie Castle?" Mr.
Pettybone's chuckle started deep in his big chest. He
closed one eye in a knowing wink. The circle of villagers on the steps of the Post Office drew more tightly
around the two figures. The big man with the red,
fleshy face and the hearty voice. The small boy with
the red hair and the slightly scared face.

"Aye," said the youngster.

"But my boy!" boomed the Secretary of the Town
Council, "there's no such thing as a ghost! *No—such—
thing!*"

"Aye," said Angus doggedly, "but there is one in Craigie Castle. I saw him myself. And talked to him."

"Dear me!" exclaimed Mr. Pettybone. "A very *friendly* ghost!" Again he winked.

"Aye," said Angus civilly.

"A friendly ghost like that should have a name," Mr. Pettybone said. "Does this—ah—ghost have a name?"

"Mr. MacSpurtle."

"Eh?" Mr. Pettybone looked startled. "Mr. who?"

"Mr. MacSpurtle!" Angus repeated. "I'm no knowing his first name."

"Dear me," exclaimed the Secretary of the Town Council. "Mr. MacSpurtle, eh? First time I ever heard of a ghost without a first name." His rich chuckle kindled a whole bonfire of chuckles from his audience. It was plain to see that Mr. Pettybone was vastly enjoying himself. "And how does this Mr. MacSpurtle of yours dress?"

"He wears the kilt."

"*Well!* A patriotic ghost too!" He waited for the laughter to die away. "Any chains?" he asked hopefully.

Angus shook his head. "Mr. MacSpurtle says that chains will be for men. Chains of pride he called them, did Mr. MacSpurtle, although it's myself is no knowing at all just what he was meaning."

Mr. Pettybone seemed to know, though. His ruddy face took on a deeper, darker flush. His hearty voice lost some of its heartiness. He said sourly, "Very strange, isn't it, that no one but you ever saw this ghost?"

"Och, but somebody did," Angus exclaimed. "Old Dugal Comrie saw him. Of course old Dugal's been dead for sixty years."

"Very convenient," sneered Mr. Pettybone. "He doesn't have many visitors, this ghost of yours."

"That's because he likes the peace and quiet," said Angus.

Again there was a chorus of quiet laughter. Only this time the villagers seemed to be laughing *at* Mr. Pettybone rather than *with* Mr. Pettybone.

The Secretary of the Town Council was getting annoyed. He wasn't used to being laughed at. Nor was he used to being bested by small boys.

"Enough of this," he snapped. "Everyone knows there's no such thing as a ghost. Science has *proved* ghosts don't exist. What do you know that the best scientists in the country don't know?"

Angus scratched his head. He wasn't quite sure how to answer Mr. Pettybone. "Maybe it's just that I know Mr. MacSpurtle, the ghost," he said simply, "and they don't."

He hadn't meant it to sound funny. But it was quite

clear from the loud laughter that everyone else *thought* it funny. Everyone, that is, except Mr. Pettybone. Mr. Pettybone looked *very* angry.

"You think you're clever, don't you? You and your stories of ghosts in kilts." He stood blusteringly over the boy. "Why don't you have the decency to admit you made the whole thing up?"

"And what about Bonnie Prince Charlie?" cut in a cool voice. "Do you think he made that up too?"

Angus wheeled around with the others when he heard the familiar voice. His heart gave a flip when he spotted the speaker. It was his friend Mr. Grant.

"I wasn't speaking to you," snapped the politician.

"No, I was speaking to you," Mr. Grant said evenly. "As a matter of fact, I asked you a question. Do you think Angus here made up that part about Prince Charlie?"

"How should I know?"

"Why not ask him?"

The big beefy man glared down at the small boy. "Well?"

Angus hesitated. Although he hadn't told Mr. Grant about Mr. MacSpurtle, it was plain that the schoolteacher had put two and two together. He said, "Mr. MacSpurtle told me everything. After all, he was there the night when Prince Charlie crossed Dunnach Moor."

Mr. Pettybone seemed to be having some sort of fit.

His face was a beet red. "That was two hundred years ago!" he roared.

"Aye, that's right, Mr. Pettybone," Angus agreed eagerly. "That's why Mr. MacSpurtle has to be more than two hundred years old himself! For if it's any less he is, then he *couldn't* have been there that night. That *proves* how old he is!"

Mr. Peter Pettybone, Secretary of the Aberdour Town Council, was not a man normally at a loss for words. Words sprang lightly and brightly to his lips and there was no end to the lightness and the brightness of them. All that was over now. He stood, shaken and mute, in the face of Angus's logic.

The words that Peter Pettybone spoke when he finally spoke them were few in number. Yet of all the words he had ever spoken none were truer than the words he now spoke.

"Feel a little like two hundred years old myself," he muttered as he walked away.

Chapter Thirteen

Angus saw Mr. MacSpurtle only briefly the following day. The little ghost sniffed when Angus told him about Mr. Pettybone.

"Them and their science! What they don't see they don't believe. And what they believe nobody *else* can see!" He sniffed.

Angus said, "And Mr. Pettybone says ye don't exist."

Mr. MacSpurtle looked hurt. "*Nobody* likes to be told he doesn't exist."

"Aye."

"It's different if ye don't exist. *Then* ye don't mind so much."

"Aye."

Mr. MacSpurtle sniffed again. "If I told Mr. Pettybone *he* didn't exist, *he* wouldn't like it either."

Angus nodded. It was easy to understand how Mr. MacSpurtle felt. To change the subject he pointed to the bagpipe under the little ghost's arm. "Ye have been practising?"

"Aye."

"Did ye—?" he began before Mr. MacSpurtle stopped him with a mournful shake of the head.

"Nothing. No a single peep out of it! Angus, Angus, do ye think I'll *ever* be able to join the rest of the MacSpurtles?" The little ghost's voice was an unhappy wail.

"Aye. Ye will," Angus said stoutly. He tried to think of something else to say that would help to cheer up his friend. He looked around at the emptiness of Dunnach Moor. It seemed to mirror the emptiness in his own heart. "At least ye do have the peace and quiet," he said hopefully.

Mr. MacSpurtle brightened a little. "That will be right, Angus. The peace and quiet of Dunnach Moor. There is no place at all in the world like it."

Angus whistled all the way home. He was glad he had been able to comfort his friend. And outside of that things were surely looking up. It was too bad, of course, that he had told anyone about Mr. MacSpurtle. Still no real harm had been done. And it *had* been grand the way things had worked out with Mr. Pettybone! He had convinced the great man he hadn't told a lie. Och, and there was no question about it. Things were very *surely* looking up!

They kept looking up too until Uncle Wull came home. Until shortly after Uncle Wull lowered his newspaper and peered at him over his glasses.

"A fine job ye did yesterday, Angus. I heard all about it today at the fishing."

"Thank ye kindly, Uncle Wull." He was delighted that his uncle should have heard how he had stood up to Mr. Pettybone. Proud too.

"It took courage," said the old man.

Angus nodded agreement. "It did that," he admitted frankly.

"When ye convinced Mr. Pettybone ye were telling the truth ye convinced everybody in Aberdour."

Something in the way Uncle Wull said the words brought Angus up short. "What will ye be meaning?" he asked.

"Och, nothing at all, lad. Just that everybody in the village is convinced there's something queer going on at Craigie Castle. Aye, maybe it's a ghost they say, and maybe not. But something *queer* just the same."

He smiled with his eyes. "It's only natural, is it no, they should want to see things for themselves?"

Angus felt his heart sink. "Ye mean, Uncle Wull, they're all going out to Craigie Castle?"

"Aye. Tomorrow it is. Mr. Pettybone will be going too."

Uncle Wull leaned forward in his chair. He pressed the tobacco into the bowl of his pipe and thrust a creased paper into the fire. His lips made a soft *popping* sound as he drew on the pipe. He studied the boy through a gentle haze of smoke.

"There will be something wrong, lad?" he asked.

Angus nodded, too stunned and sick to talk.

"Tell me about it," Uncle Wull said. "And take your time."

Under his gentle persuasion the words came out. All of them. Och, and it was the truth about Mr. Mac-Spurtle, for it's no lie he would tell at all, at all. But poor Mr. MacSpurtle was doomed to be a ghost until he got a tune out of his bagpipe. And how could he ever do that without the peace and quiet of Dunnach Moor? Aye, and little peace and quiet he would be having now with half the village of Aberdour out after him!

"Poor Mr. MacSpurtle." Angus's voice was almost a wail. "The only home he's had for the last two hundred years has been Dunnach Moor and the peace and quiet of it. And what's to become of him now? And it's all my fault."

Uncle Wull put his pipe down. He shook his head. "A bad business it is, Angus, but there's nothing ye can do about it now. Nothing at all."

Uncle Wull closed his eyes. Angus knew in his heart he was right. There was nothing he could do about it now. Nothing at all. Unless— He stopped. No, he couldn't do that. A lie was a lie. And yet—and yet—

"Uncle Wull." He didn't dare look into the old man's face.

"Aye."

"Uncle Wull, I was thinking."

"A grand way to pass the time."

He swallowed. Were ever any words so hard to speak?

"I was thinking if maybe I said—" His voice trailed away to a whisper—"that Mr. MacSpurtle *wasn't* a ghost, that maybe—" The words were too heavy to speak and there was no holding them up at all, at all. His voice died away in a small, soft chocking sound.

Uncle Wull said nothing for the longest time. Afraid to look up, Angus kept his eyes fixed on the faded red carpet on the floor. There was no sound in the room. Only the ticking of the clock. Only that and the beating of his heart. Finally, after what seemed ages, Uncle Wull spoke.

"A lie is a lie, Angus Campbell."

Angus nodded, dumbly.

"And what ye would do is a lie."

"Aye." He could feel the rough dryness of his lips when they closed in after the words.

"Ye would say there is no ghost in Craigie Castle?"

"Aye."

"And that everything ye said yesterday was a lie?"

"Aye."

"Well ye know what Aberdour would think of ye, Angus. No just the likes of Mr. Pettybone. I'm thinking of your friend Mr. Grant."

The misery was too great for his heart and he knew without caring that the smarting in his eyes was tears.

"Aye."

"And ye would still do this thing?"

"Aye." Suddenly he looked up. "It's no for myself I would do it! It's for Mr. MacSpurtle and him trusting me the way he did! And if I tell them there's no ghost in Craigie Castle and no Mr. MacSpurtle then they won't go looking for him. And if they don't go looking for him then it's the peace and quiet he will have till he joins the other MacSpurtles."

Uncle Wull sighed and put down his pipe. Slowly he got to his feet to cross to his room. He stopped when he came to Angus's chair. His hand dropped on the boy's shoulder. Angus felt the gentle pressure of the old man's fingers.

"Good lad," said Uncle Wull gruffly before he shuffled into his room. Like most Scots he dreaded any show of feeling. The awkward gesture, so rare for him, said more than any words could say.

Uncle Wull paused again when he got to the door of his room. He said gruffly again, so that the words might not sound too soft, "If a man does what he thinks is right in his heart then he will no be minding at all what the world thinks. Take that wee French lass, now, her they call Joan of Arc. Do ye think she minded at all what the world would be thinking?"

Angus shook his head miserably. "Aye, but there's a difference, Uncle Wull."

"There is?"

"I don't *feel* like Joan of Arc."

Chapter Fourteen

It had all been very fine for Joan of Arc to defy the world. Joan of Arc was a martyr. Angus Campbell wasn't. He was just a small Scottish boy trying to do what he thought was right and doing it very badly.

It had all gone off even worse than Angus had dreaded. It is not too difficult to accept ridicule. Scorn is something else again. Scorn stings with a more cutting lash. Scorn sears with a more fiery brand. And the scorn on the face of Mr. Pettybone and the others after he had told of his deceit was a cruel and terrible thing. There was no talk after that about anyone going out to Craigie Castle.

Yet if Angus had dreaded speaking to Mr. Pettybone, how much more had he dreaded speaking to Mr. Grant. For the schoolmaster was his friend. And scorn on the face of a friend cuts the heart more deeply. Still Mr. Grant had to be told. There was no question about that. But how do you go about telling a friend you had lied to him? It took Angus all of twenty-four hours to face up to the fact that Mr. Grant *had* to be told, no matter *how* he was told.

The schoolmaster, somehow, did not seem surprised when he answered the knock at the door and found the tight-faced boy standing there.

"I was wondering what had been keeping you, Angus," he said. "Come in. You'll find a few oatcakes and cheese on the table. Help yourself."

He can't know, thought Angus miserably. *If he did he would never be giving me oatcakes.*

Mr. Grant whistled as he took the tartan tea cozy off the pot. He poured the well-brewed tea into the big mug.

"Nothing like a cup of tea, Angus." He smiled. "A cup of tea and an oatcake. They're a grand pair."

Och, and he can't know! Yet all Aberdour must know. Even old Malcolm Fraser had finally heard about it. And how could old Malcolm know and not

Mr. Grant? Yet there he sits pouring out the tea as though nothing had happened.

Angus wet his lips. It was better that he spoke up now. Better now than after he had eaten Mr. Grant's oatcakes.

"I have something to tell ye," he said.

The schoolmaster didn't look up as he spread the butter on the oatcake. "If it's about there being no ghost in Craigie Castle, don't bother. I heard all about it." He glanced up. "How thick a piece of cheese do you want?"

Angus stared. "But you're no angry at all?"

"Angry? Why should I be angry?"

"But—but the thing I told them—"

The schoolmaster moved his shoulders in a shrug. "It's not what we tell others that matters, Angus. It's what we tell ourselves." He munched on his oatcake and sipped his tea. "And if what we tell ourselves is the truth, then why worry what the world thinks?"

"Ye mean," whispered Angus, "like Joan of Arc? The French lassie?"

Mr. Grant looked puzzled for a moment, then smiled. "You might say that." He paused. "There's just one thing I don't understand."

"And what would that be, Mr. Grant?"

"Why did you tell everyone there was no ghost in

the castle? You believed there was. Why did **you** change your story?"

"Och, Mr. Grant, I just had to! They were all going out after him, Mr. Pettybone and the rest of them. How could he hide from them? And where could he go, for there's no place like Dunnach Moor for the peace and quiet. So I told them there was no ghost at all. I told them there was no Mr. MacSpurtle." His voice choked. "I told them I had made it all up."

Mr. Grant shook his head and put down his cup. "Poor wee Angus. So you went through all this for your friend, Mr. MacSpurtle?"

Angus nodded.

The schoolmaster put his arm around the boy's shoulder. "Poor wee Angus," he said again. He suddenly frowned. "It was strange, though, how everybody believed you when you said there *was* no Mr. MacSpurtle."

Angus looked at him curiously, "And why, Mr. Grant?"

"Because if there's no Mr. MacSpurtle then how did you know about Bonnie Prince Charlie and Dunnach Moor? *Someone* told you these things, Angus. No one in Aberdour knew them." He paused. "It *was* Mr. Mac-Spurtle, wasn't it?"

Angus nodded. "Aye it was. And it was himself knew these things because he was there that night."

The schoolmaster walked quietly over to the window. For a long moment he stared out, lost in thought. He said slowly, "Who or what this Mr. MacSpurtle is I cannot say. That he knows things that we do not, there is no denying. How he learned these things we do not know either. A strange and uncanny knowledge of the past has your Mr. MacSpurtle." He paused and turning his eyes away from the window looked hard at Angus. "Among other things of the past."

Angus said, "What will ye be meaning, Mr. Grant?"

"Did you buy a chocolate bar the other day?"

"Aye."

"In Mrs. Simpson's?"

"Aye." What on earth was Mr. Grant getting at?

"And did you give her a silver coin for it?"

Angus frowned. "Aye, I did."

The schoolmaster suddenly put his hand in his pocket. "*This* one?"

Angus took the coin from the outstretched hand. He stared at it. It wasn't a shilling. And it wasn't a half crown. He had never seen a coin quite like it. Or had he? There was something oddly familiar about it. . . .

"That's a guinea, Angus," Mr. Grant said quietly.

"A—a what?"

"A guinea."

"A guinea? But—but everybody knows a guinea is

twenty-one shillings and that there's no coin for it at all!"

Mr. Grant said in the same quiet voice, "That's a *special* kind of guinea. It's called a Queen Anne guinea. It's not in use any more."

Angus knew the answer before he whispered the question. "And when was it in use?"

"It was in use when Bonnie Prince Charlie crossed over to Scotland from France."

Angus looked at it in awe. It was smooth and worn and a strange heaviness in his hand. Mr. Grant's voice seemed to come from miles—from ages—away.

"Mrs. Simpson didn't notice at the time who had given her this coin. But afterward it came back to her. She said *you* gave it to her, Angus."

"But where would I get—" He stopped. All of a sudden he remembered. Mr. MacSpurtle! That first time they had met. *Here's something for ye, laddie. For sweeties.* Was this the coin he had given him? He had not looked at it. It might and again it might not be. But if it wasn't, how had it come to be in his pocket?

"Mr. MacSpurtle gave you that coin, didn't he, Angus?"

"I—I don't know. He—he gave me a coin. *For sweeties* he said. I didn't look at it at all. I never thought to look."

"Still, it does look very much as though this rare

Queen Anne guinea came from Mr. MacSpurtle, doesn't it?"

Angus nodded. He suddenly thought of something. "Will there be anybody else besides ye and Mrs. Simpson—?"

"This is Aberdour, Angus. *Everybody* knows about it. Old Malcolm Fraser got the news himself half an hour ago."

There was something wrong. He could tell it by the queer way Mr. Grant was looking at him.

"It's just this, Angus. The villagers are sure now that something strange is going on around Craigie Castle. Mr. Pettybone naturally said it was all very simple. He said you had somehow found this coin and most likely others also, in Craigie Castle. To keep others away you told the story about the ghost. When you found out they were going anyway, you told the second story of there being no ghost. Mr. Pettybone is very sure of these theories, Angus, for after all, *he* thought them up. So right at this minute he's on his way with five of his cronies to Craigie Castle."

Angus stared at him. It was impossible. It couldn't be true. It just *couldn't.*

Mr. Grant said quietly, "I'm rather afraid that your mysterious little friend, Mr. MacSpurtle, has seen the end of his peace and quiet."

The first few words were all that Angus heard before he realized what had to be done. And done quickly.

"Thank ye kindly, Mr. Grant!" he cried as he leaped to his feet. "For the oatcake and everything!"

The schoolmaster opened his mouth to say something but Angus never heard it.

He was already out of the door and running as fast as he had ever run toward Craigie Castle.

Chapter Fifteen

There was a fierce burning in his lungs. His chest heaved with pain. He drove his legs, leaden with weariness, through the heather. Yet he had to keep on running. Only by running could he hope to get there before the others. Only by running could he try to warn Mr. MacSpurtle.

It was hopeless. He knew it. Knew it with every *thump, thump, thump* of his heart. He could never really hope to reach the castle before Mr. Pettybone and the others. No matter how hard he ran. Perhaps they would surprise Mr. MacSpurtle strolling outside

the castle. The thought made Angus sick. Poor Mr. MacSpurtle. Thinking himself alone in the middle of Dunnach Moor and the peace and quiet of it. Poor Mr. MacSpurtle!

He was past the black waters of the loch now. *Thump, thump, thump* beat his heart against his ribs. *Thump, thump, thump* fell his feet in the tufts of purple heather. And now he could see them. Six tiny specks in the distance. But och, so far away! He could never reach them before they got to the castle. Never! Never! Never!

Tears stung his eyes, yet he never slackened his pace. Headlong he dashed across the moor. "Mr. Mac-Spurtle! Mr. MacSpurtle!" he kept crying, hoping somehow to warn his little friend. "Mr. MacSpurtle! Mr. MacSpurtle!" And all the time he cried the words the wind blowing in his face bent them back and filled his ears with the sound of them. "Mr. Mac-Spurtle! Mr. MacSpurtle! Mr. MacSpurtle!"

They were only about a quarter of a mile ahead of him now and drawing close to the castle. He could make out the big figure of Mr. Pettybone in front with the other five scattered out behind him. Steadily they moved toward the big gate. The only sign of life in all of Dunnach Moor. One big figure in front. Five others at his heels. And a small, red-headed boy far behind.

Suddenly, there was a stir in the heather just ahead of Mr. Pettybone. Angus saw the villagers freeze, then heard their shrill cries. At the same moment he caught a glimpse of a tiny figure in full flight toward the castle. A tiny figure, bent low and scurrying from cover to cover. The next moment the villagers, with Mr. Pettybone in the lead, were in full chase after it.

"Mr. MacSpurtle! Och, Mr. MacSpurtle!" Angus wailed as he ran. He was sure it had been Mr. MacSpurtle despite the fact he had not seen his face. Poor Mr. MacSpurtle, out for a stroll and enjoying the peace and quiet of Dunnach Moor. He prayed they would not catch him.

He could hear Mr. Pettybone's deep voice baying commands to the others. He did not see Mr. MacSpurtle after that. With the Secretary of the Town Council charging ahead, the villagers burst through the gate of Craigie Castle. He could only hope that Mr. MacSpurtle had somehow escaped them.

He was only a hundred yards away from the castle when he heard it. A thin, high wail that brought him to a dead halt. He stood, his chest heaving, a wonder in his eyes. It was like no other sound Angus had ever heard. A shrill, reedy sob rising and falling, rising and falling. Slowly the strange sounds took on a form, a pattern. Slowly the notes struggled into place. He held his breath. It couldn't be—it just couldn't—but it was! The bagpipes!

It was a lament. A *coronach* for the dead. Mournfully the notes drifted out from the castle. They seemed to flap in the air like tired banners. And tired banners they were, the banners of the mighty clan MacSpurtle trooping for the last time as the last of the MacSpurtles played them to rest.

Angus felt tears thicken in his eyes. And whether they were tears of joy or tears of sadness it would have been hard for him to say. For Mr. MacSpurtle was going away. Going away from Dunnach Moor to that place where he longed to be. Angus never moved from where he stood until the last thin notes had trembled to rest in the air.

How had he done it? How had Mr. MacSpurtle succeeded at last in playing his pipes? Then all of a sudden Angus saw the scene before his eyes. The little figure fleeing as fast as it could go before the charge of Mr. Pettybone and the villagers. With his beloved castle under attack, Mr. MacSpurtle had reached for the only weapon left him, his bagpipe. For it was with the skirl of the pipes in their ears that the Highland warriors had always gone into battle. Panting, he had thrust the blow pipe to his lips. His scrawny chest, heavy with air, had pumped the tartan bag full. And after two hundred years Mr. MacSpurtle had played the pipes!

That was how it had happened. He was sure of it. And the knowledge of it filled him with a strange and a wonderful peace. He would miss Mr. MacSpurtle with his funny smile and his bright blue eyes. He was glad, though, that the little ghost had finally gone on to that place where he had yearned to be, where the peace and the quiet was no less than the peace and quiet of his beloved Dunnach Moor.

It was a full hour later that Mr. Pettybone and the others trudged out of the castle. The Secretary of the Town Council looked angry. His beefy face was red and perspired. He had a cut over his right eye. His trousers were ripped and dusty. He was limping. It was rather plain to see that he had not been as sure-footed as Mr. MacSpurtle in getting around the castle!

"It's hurt your head is, Mr. Pettybone," Angus said with a cluck of sympathy.

Mr. Pettybone scowled. "Thanks for reminding me," he snapped. He dabbed at the cut over his eye with a big handkerchief. "Almost killed myself in there. Rocks all over the place." He grunted. "You see anybody come out of the castle?"

"No," Angus said truthfully.

Mr. Pettybone grunted again. "Probably some gypsy or poacher. Just got a glimpse of him. Couldn't have

been more than four feet tall. The fellow ran like a rabbit."

"What would a poacher be doing here?" asked Ian Menzies, one of the villagers.

"Hiding out," snapped Mr. Pettybone impatiently.

Ian nodded uncertainly. Plainly he didn't agree with Mr. Pettybone. Yet plainly he wasn't going to argue the point with the Secretary of the Town Council.

"And that queer noise we heard," he muttered. He looked back uneasily at the castle. "Wonder what it was?"

"The wind," said Mr. Pettybone, never at a loss for an answer. "All these old places have echo chambers. What do you think it was anyway?"

Ian scratched his head. "I don't know, Mr. Pettybone," he said thoughtfully. "Almost sounded like some kind of bagpipe."

Mr. Pettybone snorted with disgust. "You call that bagpipe music? You start playing like that, Ian Menzies, and you'll lose that job you have on the Aberdour Pipe Band."

Ian nodded hastily. "I didn't say it *was* bagpipe music, Mr. Pettybone. After all, who would be playing the bagpipes in an empty castle?"

Mr. Pettybone in a grunting mood, grunted again. He placed his big hand tenderly on his wrenched knee and winced with pain.

"Och, and it's hurt your knee is too!" Angus cried with concern.

Mr. Pettybone glared at him. "Thanks to you! If I hadn't listened to you I'd never have come here!"

"But—"

"*Anyway*," Mr. Pettybone said with a growl, "I'm satisfied about one thing. We've gone through Craigie Castle from top to bottom. There's nothing there." He glared again at the boy. "And that goes for ghosts too."

Angus nodded. He felt sorry for poor Mr. Pettybone. He looked so unhappy. And how would he *ever* be able to limp all the way back across Dunnach Moor? He was pleased, therefore, that he could agree with him so easily.

"That's true, Mr. Pettybone," he said with a bright smile. "There's no ghost at all in Craigie Castle—now."